# FAMILY BUSINESS

# SUDDENLY ROYAL

# FAMILY BUSINESS

VANESSA ACTON

darbycreek

MINNEAPOLIS

Darby Creek
A division of Lerner Publishing Group, Inc.
241 First Avenue North
Minneapolis, MN 55401 USA

For reading levels and more information, look up this title at
www.lernerbooks.com.

Cover and interior images: Igor Klimov/Shutterstock.com (background texture); GoMixer/Shutterstock.com (coat of arms and lion); KazanovskyAndrey/iStock/Getty Images Plus (gold); mona redshinestudio/Shutterstock.com (crown).

Main body text set in Janson Text LT Std 12/17.5.
Typeface provided by Adobe Systems.


**Library of Congress Cataloging-in-Publication Data**

Names: Acton, Vanessa, author.
Title: Family business / Vanessa Acton.
Description: Minneapolis : Darby Creek, [2018] | Series: Suddenly royal | Summary: Mel, seventeen, has always wondered about her father, but is surprised to learn he is a member of the Evonian nobility and that he wants her to visit him and his family.
Identifiers: LCCN 2018001958 (print) | LCCN 2018009462 (ebook) | ISBN 9781541525948 (eb pdf) | ISBN 9781541525689 (lb : alk. paper) | ISBN 9781541526372 (pb : alk. paper)
Subjects: | CYAC: Nobility—Fiction. | Fathers and daughters—Fiction. | Stepmothers—Fiction. | Identity—Fiction.
Classification: LCC PZ7.1.A228 (ebook) | LCC PZ7.1.A228 Fam 2018 (print) | DDC [Fic]—dc23

LC record available at https://lccn.loc.gov/2018001958

Manufactured in the United States of America
1-44552-35483-4/2/2018

to A.J., for fixing
all the words

# The Valmont Family of Evonia

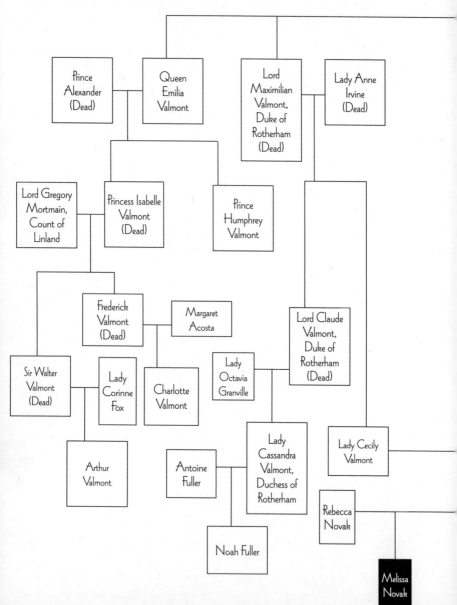

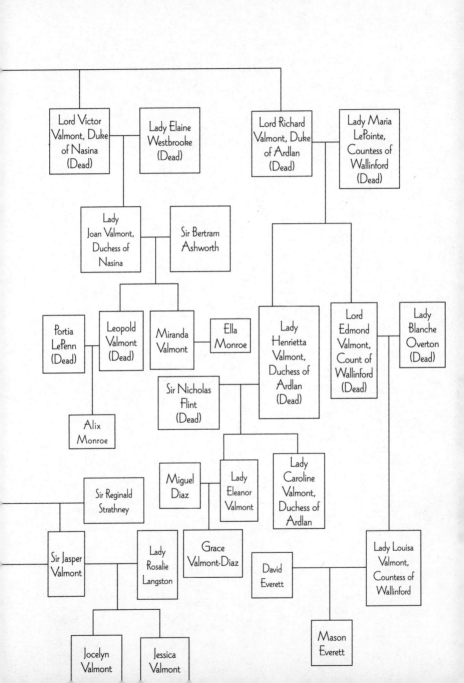

# 1

Mel was cleaning up her mom's room when she found the letter. Her mom was on a date with What's His Name. (Mel knew his name was Todd but didn't like to admit she was paying any attention to her mom's dating life.) Since Mel herself hadn't made any plans that night, she decided to do what she usually did when she was annoyed at her mom: clean up after her.

So there Mel was at nine o'clock on the first Tuesday in June, rummaging through her mom's dresser. She knew she was probably overstepping, but the dresser desperately needed to be straightened up. Every drawer was crammed with makeup, jewelry, clothes, receipts, tax documents . . .

As Mel reached to the very back of the middle drawer, she found an envelope pinned behind a jumble of underwear. When her fingers brushed the paper, Mel thought it might be a bill. One of the credit card companies still sent paper statements, which was actually kind of nice because her mom often forgot to check the balance online.

Mel got hold of the edge of the bill and dragged it to freedom. But it wasn't a bill—it was a letter. And it was addressed to Ms. Rebecca Novak, Mel's mom, in elegant script that Mel could barely read. An elaborate return address label sat on the envelope's top left corner:

*Sir Jasper Valmont*
*33 Darnley Place*
*Alaborn, Evonia 05550 EV*

Evonia? Where was that? Some alternate universe where people still sent written letters instead of emails?

Curious, Mel turned over the envelope. It had already been opened. Mel found herself pulling out the letter. And then unfolding it. And then reading the handwritten message on it.

*Dear Becca,*

*I wanted to say this last week, but I couldn't find the words. I'm so sorry that things had to end this way—sorry that they had to end at all. These last three years have meant so much to me, and I'll never forget you. Of course, you have every right to be angry. This is unfair to you in so many ways. I hope someday you'll forgive me. But mostly I hope you'll find happiness. You deserve it more than anyone I know.*

*With love,*
*Jasper*

There was a date in the top corner of the page. The letter had been written the year before Mel was born. In fact—Mel did some quick counting—*eight months* before she was born.

Mel took a deep, shaky breath. Her mom's story had always been the same. *My twenties were pretty wild. I don't know who your dad was. But I can guarantee that he wasn't someone you'd want to meet.*

But here was this guy, Jasper, talking about being in a relationship with Mel's mom for *three years*. And he'd broken up with her right after Mel's mom would've gotten pregnant. Of course it was possible that Mel's mom had cheated on this guy. But if that had happened, Jasper didn't seem to have known about it. His letter made it clear that he didn't blame Mel's mom for the breakup.

Besides, Mel knew her mom well enough to know that she wasn't a good enough multi-tasker to juggle more than one guy at a time. These days she could barely manage to fit Todd into her schedule. Though she did keep dropping hints about wanting Mel to meet him. Just the idea made Mel grimace. What's His Name sounded like a fine guy, but her mom's relationships usually only lasted a few months. Mel didn't see much point in getting to know someone who would probably be gone soon. She didn't need a father-figure replacement in her life anymore.

On the other hand, if her *actual* father entered the picture . . . well, that would be different.

\*\*\*

When Mel's mom came home that night, Mel was sprawled on the living room couch, pretending to watch TV. "Hey, Mom. How was your night?"

Her mom beamed at her. "It was lovely! I can't wait for you to meet Todd, I know you'll hit it off—"

Mel cleared her throat to cut off her mom. She really didn't want to hear about What's His Name right now. "Um, yeah, so, here's the thing. You know how you asked me to vacuum? Well, I did, and—"

"Oh, thanks, honey. I would've done it myself, but between work and tonight's plans I just completely ran out of—"

"I also decided to straighten up some other

stuff while I was at it, and . . . I found this." Mel held up the letter. "I know I probably shouldn't have read it, but . . ."

The color drained from her mom's face as she took the letter from Mel's hands.

"Oh . . . oh, Mel. I—wow, I didn't even realize I still had this letter."

"So this Jasper Valmont . . . would you say he's, um, a strong candidate for being my dad?"

Mel's mom collapsed onto the couch and swore softly under her breath. "This is not how I wanted you to find out about him."

"Is that a yes?"

"I'm so sorry I didn't tell you about this sooner. It just didn't seem like a burden you needed to carry."

"That sounds like a yes."

Her mom let out a rough sigh. "Jasper Valmont is definitely your father, sweetheart."

Mel had thought that hearing her mom confirm it would come as a relief. But instead she just felt more tense and agitated than ever. Her mom had been *lying* to her all these years. "And you never told me about this because. . . ?"

"Because—okay, just bear with me here. Jasper is from Evonia, which is—"

"A tiny country in Europe," Mel cut in. She held up her phone. "I looked it up while I was waiting for you to get home. I didn't know you'd ever been to Europe."

"I haven't. Jasper and I met while he was going to grad school in the States. We were together for a few years, but eventually he broke things off because his parents didn't approve of me. He made the decision very suddenly and moved back to Evonia right after the breakup. I was so angry—so blindsided, honestly—that I cut off contact with him completely. Then, right after that, I realized I was pregnant, but I decided not to tell him. I didn't want him to think I was trying to trap him into staying with me. His parents definitely would've assumed I was some kind of gold digger who wanted him to marry me. And at that point, I didn't even want to speak to him again. So I didn't."

"Not even after you got that letter," Mel said quietly.

"Especially not after I got the letter."
Her mom's tone twisted with bitterness. "This
is the most halfhearted, self-serving . . . ugh."

Mel picked at a loose thread on the couch
cushion. "I mean, I thought it was kinda
romantic."

Her mom shook her head and tossed the
letter onto the cluttered coffee table a little
more forcefully than necessary. "It's the kind
of apology people write when they want to
make *themselves* feel better. He knew what he
was doing when he ended things. He knew he
was being cowardly. Apologizing for it after the
fact isn't worth much."

Mel wasn't sure she agreed, but she had
so many other questions she wanted her
mom to answer that it wasn't worth arguing
over now. "So why didn't his parents approve
of you?"

Mel's mom heaved another sigh. "Because
they're royalty."

"Yeah," said Mel flatly, waving her phone
in the air again. "I came across that little
tidbit too."

Jasper Valmont was not a very common name. Mel had found him online immediately. He was a middle-aged guy, good-looking in a low-key way, with the same hair color, eye color, and face shape as Mel. He lived in Evonia, sat on the board of several nonprofit organizations Mel had never heard of, and seemed to be married. In several of the photos floating around online, he was with the same very pretty woman. A woman who looked as if she'd never seen a mess in her life, much less made one.

While she was initially surprised by her father's status, a few more internet searches had given Mel enough of a basic understanding

of the Evonian royal family to know that—
barring some major disasters—she wasn't in
danger of becoming the daughter of a king.
Jasper Valmont was the great-nephew of
Evonia's queen. The queen didn't have any
political power, but she and her relatives were
wealthy, famous in their home country, and
extremely fond of tradition.

Mel's mom picked up where Mel's research
had left off. Jasper's parents had wanted him
to marry someone of a similar background—
upper class, part of a noble family. Rebecca
Novak, an American nursing student, didn't
fit the bill.

"And you're sure they wouldn't have
changed their minds if they'd known about
me?" Mel pressed. She was trying very hard
to be mature about this—resisting the urge to
yell at her mom for keeping such a huge secret
from her. But she knew her voice already had
an edge to it that gave away how angry she was.

"They wouldn't have changed their minds
about *me*," Mel's mom said firmly. "They might
have decided Jasper and I should get married,

but they wouldn't have been happy about it. And I didn't necessarily *want* to marry Jasper, even before he caved to his parents' demands and treated me like dirt."

Mel wrinkled her nose. "But you just explained how *you* felt and what *you* wanted. What about me? Didn't it ever occur you to that I might want a relationship with my dad? Like when I was little and I asked you a zillion times if you had any guesses about who he was? Or in elementary school when I went through that phase of telling my friends that my dad was a spy who was always away on secret missions? Or—"

"I admit I probably should've said something sooner. I just wanted to wait until you were old enough to . . ." Her mom trailed off.

"Old enough to what? Not care about it?" Mel's voice rose. Her not-yelling plan was unraveling fast.

Mel's mom opened her mouth, then closed it and clenched her jaw. "Old enough to not be crushed if you reached out to him and he didn't want anything to do with you."

Mel's stomach did a long, slow, painful roll. "So you don't think he would want to know about me?"

"I honestly have no idea, Mel. I haven't been in touch with him in almost eighteen years. I don't know if he's still the person I remember. Maybe he *would* want to be in contact with you. I just want you to be prepared for the possibility that he wouldn't."

Mel reached over and picked up the letter her mom had left on the coffee table. The guy who'd written this letter had seemed genuinely pained about the breakup—had seemed to really want to do the right thing. She had a hard time believing that this guy would brush her off if he found out about her.

"If you do want to try to get in touch with him, I'm not going to stop you," her mom went on. Her voice was weary. "I can probably even get you his old email address if I dig back far enough. While we were together, we used to email whenever he went back to visit Evonia. I don't know if the address still works, but—"

"I'd like to try it," Mel said instantly.

"Okay. Tomorrow. After we've both gotten some sleep."

* * *

The next morning, Mel paced from one end of her bedroom to the other while her best friends, Savannah and Elise, stood at her desk staring at her laptop. They were reading the email Mel had drafted. After spending forty minutes typing variations of "Hello, Sir Jasper, my name is Melissa Novak," Mel had finally pounded out a full message.

After explaining that Rebecca Novak was her mother and they were pretty sure he was her father, she covered the other bases: *I'm attaching a scanned copy of the letter you wrote to my mom a few months before I was born, plus a photo of myself so you can see what I look like. I'd be happy to have a paternity test done if you feel you need proof of our relationship. I'm not looking for money. Neither is my mom. I just thought I'd let you know I'm out here, in case you'd like to be in touch with me.*

Savannah and Elise had clearly read through the draft several times by now. But they still hadn't said anything. "What do you think?" Mel finally burst out.

"I think it's good," said Savannah. "No typos."

"I think you should attach more photos," Elise suggested. "So he knows you didn't just find some random internet photo of a girl who looks like him."

"Good point," said Mel. She stopped pacing and stood directly behind them, facing her laptop screen. "But it doesn't sound sketchy or anything?"

"It sounds very legit," Elise assured her.

"Cool, cool. I'll add some more photos and then I'll—"

"Just go ahead and send it now," said Savannah. "You can always send him more stuff later if he asks for it."

"If he responds at all, you mean."

"You don't think he will?" asked Elise.

Mel shrugged, trying to look casual. "My mom doesn't think he will. I can tell."

"Well, I understand why she feels that way," said Elise. "This dude dumped her because she wasn't from a rich, important family."

"Yeah, but *she's* the one who lied to me about it." Mel knew she sounded bitter and could tell that her friends weren't sure how to react. They were used to hearing Mel complain about her mom, but they'd never seen her get truly furious at her mom before.

"Yeah," sighed Savannah. "But I mean, if he's trash, I kind of don't blame her."

"He's not trash," Mel snapped. "I can tell, okay?"

"It's his parents who are trash, right?" added Elise. "Lord and Lady Blah-Blah-Blah pressured him into breaking up with your mom."

"Sir Reginald Strathney and Lady Cecily Valmont," Mel recited, nodding. "Yeah. They're the ones who are really to blame."

"If his dad's last name is Strathney, how come *his* last name is Valmont?" asked Elise.

Mel shrugged. "My mom said it has something to do with the royal name being passed down through every branch of the family." She'd thought about last names a lot in the past twelve hours. Thought about what it would've been like to be Melissa Valmont instead of Melissa Novak.

"Okay, focus," said Savannah. "Send the email first, *then* get hung up on his family's weird naming conventions."

"Right. Okay." Mel sat down and stared at her message, the cursor hovering over SEND, her finger inches from the touch pad. Seconds ticked by.

Finally Savannah gently bumped Mel's hand. "There! Done. Now all you can do is wait."

\*\*\*

She didn't have to wait long. A response was in her inbox the next morning.

*Hello Melissa,*

*Well, this is certainly a surprise. Thank you for your email and the photo. I do clearly see the family resemblance, and everything about the timeline adds up. I don't believe a paternity test will be necessary. In return, I've attached a recent picture of me with my wife, Rosalie, and our two daughters. Jocelyn is twelve and Jessica is ten . . .*

Mel immediately clicked on the attachment. And there they were, posing in some sort of fancy garden: Jasper, the pretty dark-haired lady, and two girls who looked eerily like Mel. The older one had thick bangs that Mel knew the girl would regret in a few years, and the younger one had more freckles than Mel had ever seen on one person. But other than that, they could've been younger versions of Mel. *Jocelyn and Jessica—he gave them both "J" names*, she found herself thinking. *That's . . . cute, I guess?*

After staring at the girls for a minute, she went back to reading the email:

*I'm sure you have countless questions. I'd be happy to talk with you over the phone or via video chat. I believe we're about seven hours ahead of you . . .*

Mel skimmed down to the end of the email, her eyes landing on the signature.

*Sincerely,*
*Jasper*

Mel exhaled slowly. Somehow this didn't feel as momentous as she'd expected. It wasn't a letdown, exactly, but she'd been hoping for . . . well, she wasn't sure what. He believed that she was his daughter, and he wanted to talk to her. In fact, he was being amazingly chill about this whole situation. Shouldn't that be more than enough to satisfy her?

She pulled up the photo of Jasper and his family again. They looked so stiff and formal—nothing like the way Mel and her mom posed for photos, making goofy faces or barely holding back snorts of laughter. These people were smiling with their mouths closed, their eyes staring blankly straight ahead. To Mel, they didn't look like a real family. She couldn't picture her mom posed in the same awkward way.

Looking back at the email, Mel realized why she felt so oddly disappointed. She'd been hoping that he would be overjoyed to find out about her *and* gutted with regret over the time they'd lost. Instead she'd gotten polite acceptance and an offer to set up a video chat.

But it was better than nothing.

***

The image on Mel's laptop screen was fuzzy and kept freezing up, but the sound quality wasn't too bad. "Hello, Melissa," said Jasper Valmont. He had a light accent that sounded like a cross between British and French. "I'm . . . glad we were able to make this happen." He sounded as if he were trying to remember a script he'd memorized. And he didn't seem to be smiling, but it was hard to be sure when the video was so sketchy.

"Me too," said Mel. She smiled extra wide so it would be obvious. "And you can call me Mel—everyone else does. And I guess I should call you . . ."

"Just Jasper is fine. No need for formalities."

"Oh. Okay." She guessed she should be glad he wasn't insisting on *Sir* Jasper. "So it's, like, early evening over there, right?"

"Yes, just about time for supper. And it's late morning where you are?"

"Yep, just about time for . . . a random snack, probably." *Great, we're talking about time zones and meals. Not exactly an inspiring start to this conversation.*

"And what are you up to today?"

"Not much—I'm hanging out with some friends later. I'm on summer vacation until the beginning of September." *Why does everything I'm saying sound so boring? Why does my LIFE sound so boring? I'm interesting, Jasper, I promise!*

"Well, speaking of that—I was wondering. Would you be interested in visiting me in Evonia for a couple of weeks later this summer? I could cover the cost of your plane ticket, and that would give us a chance to get to know each other."

Mel's plastered-on grin suddenly became genuine. "Really? Your family would be okay with that?"

"Ro and the girls would love to meet you."

*Ugh, Ro and the girls.* Mel hoped this wasn't going to turn into some sort of fairy tale situation, with a wicked stepmother and stepsisters trying to make her life miserable. Technically, Jocelyn and Jessica were her *half* sisters, but that didn't guarantee they'd be likeable.

Still, she couldn't pass up a chance to spend time with her father.

"In that case," she said, "I'm in."

3

"I wish you'd checked with me first before you agreed to something like that," Mel's mom said to her.

"Yeah, well, I wish you'd checked with me before you decided to keep my father's identity a secret for seventeen years," Mel snapped back before she could stop herself.

Mel's mom was quiet for a moment. Mel could tell she was biting the insides of her mouth to keep from blurting out a retort. Finally her mom said, "It's just that you'll need a passport, and it can take a couple months for an application to get processed . . ."

"Oh, so that's what's bothering you? The logistics of me traveling to Europe?" Mel knew she was just going to make this situation worse, but she couldn't seem to stop herself. "Not, you know, the fact that my dad actually *does* want to get to know me? Not the fact that you were wrong about him all this time?"

Her mom crossed her arms and leveled Mel with a surprisingly intimidating stare. Suddenly she didn't look like easygoing Becca Novak anymore. She looked truly angry. "You know, I didn't give you a hard time for snooping through my stuff without my permission. And I helped you get in contact with Jasper when you said that was what you wanted. And I'm not saying you can't go to Europe. If I'm supposed to be the terrible mother who kept you away from your magical, perfect, royal father all these years, I have an interesting way of going about it, don't you think?"

Mel's eyes stung. She looked away. "I don't think you're a terrible mother. But I *do* think I'm allowed to be upset that I never had a chance to meet him until now."

Her mom sighed. "You're allowed to feel however you feel, Mel. And I'm glad that Jasper wants to be part of your life—I really am. But back when we broke up, I made the choice that I thought would be best for everyone, and I can't undo that choice now. I'm not asking you to agree with me, I'm just asking you to respect that I was doing my best. I've always wanted what's best for you."

"I know that, Mom. I do." Mel took a deep breath. "But now it's time for me to decide what's best for me. And that's going to Evonia and visiting my dad." After a short pause, she added, "So how do I apply for a passport?"

\*\*\*

Two months later, Mel stepped out of a car in Alaborn, Evonia's capital city, and stared at the elegant three-story brick house in front of her: 33 Darnley Place. Jasper Valmont's home. She pulled out her phone, noticing that her hands were shaking. First she shot off a message to her mom: *Just got here.* Then she messaged Savannah and Elise, even though Evonia was eight time zones away from home and her friends were probably still asleep: *Made it—standing in front of the house. Suddenly terrified.*

The driver of the car got her duffel bag out of the trunk and brought it over to her. He said, "You can go right in, Miss Novak," which was what he'd been calling her ever since he picked her up from the airport. Apparently he was Jasper's personal driver. His name was LaRue—he wouldn't tell her his first name. Or anything else. She'd tried making conversation during the drive into Evonia. But he had just turned the radio to some sort of weird Euro-pop station and responded to her questions with either "I wouldn't know about that, Miss Novak" or "I'm sure your father will have more to say about that, Miss Novak."

Now she was here. And LaRue was telling her to go in. "Thanks," she said to him, shouldering her duffel bag with one hand and still clutching her phone with the other. She took a deep breath and walked up the front steps. Then, just as she was wondering whether to put her phone in her pocket or set down her bag so that she'd have one hand free to ring the bell, the door swung open.

A pudgy man dressed in a crisp black suit stood in the doorway. This was not her dad. This was—the butler? "Good afternoon, Miss Novak," he said. "Welcome to Darnley Place. I'll inform the family that you've arrived."

"Um, thank you," she said as he stepped aside and ushered her into the entryway. "Sorry, I don't know your name . . . ?"

"Baines, miss. I'm Sir Jasper's butler." *Ha! I was right. One point for me.* "Wait here for just one moment."

He knocked on a door that led off from the entryway, and Jasper Valmont's voice called "Come in!" Baines cracked the door open and announced, "Miss Melissa Novak, sir."

A woman's voice said, "Oh good! Thank you, Baines. Send her in."

Baines opened the door all the way and made a sweeping gesture with his arm that Mel interpreted as "Go ahead." She hastily put her phone away, adjusted her grip on her duffel bag, and walked into the room.

Mel's eyes went into sensory overload, trying to take in everything at once. The room had a grand brick fireplace, towering bookcases, and thick curtains and rugs. Jasper was sitting in an armchair with an open book in his lap, his wife was getting up from the sofa, and her two half sisters were kneeling on the floor with a complicated-looking board game spread out between them. Everyone and *everything* seemed to be staring at her.

"Hello, Melissa!" said the woman brightly, coming toward her. "It's lovely to have you here. I'm Ro." Mel braced herself for an uncomfortable hug or a sickly-sweet kiss on the cheek. But instead Ro simply held out her hand for Mel to shake.

"Hi, Ro. You can actually call me Mel," Mel said as she shook her stepmother's hand. Ro had a firm grip, but not a crushing one. And her smile seemed sincere. "It's nice to be here."

She looked past Ro to Jasper, who had finally set his book down and gotten up from his chair. "Yes," he said, nodding at her. Not smiling, not holding out his arms for a hug or even a handshake, just standing there and nodding. "Yes, very glad to have you. How was the flight?"

Mel shrugged, then realized that she was still holding her duffel bag and that her arm and shoulder were starting to ache. She gently set the bag on the floor. "I slept through most of it, so if there were any problems, I missed them." This didn't get much of a reaction from Jasper. He just kept nodding, though Ro gave a gentle, polite chuckle.

"That's the best anyone can hope for on such a long flight," Ro said. "Girls, come over here and meet your sister."

The two girls got up off the floor and came over to stand next to Ro. They were both wearing skirts and light sweaters that didn't quite match but had clearly come from the same high-end store. Mel imagined it was called *Awkward Tween Fashions*. "This is Joss," Ro said, putting her hand on the shoulder of the taller girl, "and this is Jess." The younger girl stuck out her hand just like her mother had. Mel shook it.

"Hi," said Mel.

"Very pleased to meet you," said both J-kids in creepy unison.

"Your ponytail is crooked," added the older J-kid matter-of-factly.

*Wow, great start.* "Yeah, like I said, I slept for most of my flight. I haven't had time to dress for the occasion. Not exactly ready for a formal ball or anything. I hope that's not the first thing on the agenda?"

Once again, only Ro reacted to Mel's attempt at a joke. With another polite laugh, she said, "No, the first thing on the agenda was to let you get settled in. Are you hungry? Airplane food can be so hit or miss."

"I'm starving, actually," Mel admitted.

"That's because of the jetlag," said the older J-kid—Joss. *The older one has the "o" in her name*, Mel reminded herself. *"O" for older. "O" for knOw-it-all.*

"Actually I'm *always* starving," Mel said, keeping her tone light and her face smiley even though she would've liked to shoot the girl a glare.

"I've heard that Americans tend to be hungry all the time," said Joss without missing a beat.

"Oh yeah," Mel said. "We'll eat anything. Jumbo burgers, entire racks of prime rib, little girls . . ."

This time even Ro didn't try to laugh. The Js looked at Mel thoughtfully. Then Jess said, "Lucky there are no *little* girls here," and Jasper cleared his throat loudly.

"Shall we go to Bellamy's for afternoon tea then?" he suggested. Both Js instantly nodded.

"Who's Bellamy?" Mel asked.

Joss shot her another know-it-all look. "It's one of the oldest and best restaurants in Alaborn."

"Oh, right. Sounds great." *Get me out of here*, she thought. *Or at least get me away from these judgmental kids so I can spend some quality time with the person who actually matters.*

But Ro was already saying that she'd have LaRue bring the car back around and they'd all meet in the front hall in fifteen minutes. She turned to Mel and told her that she'd show Mel her room in the meantime. So about ten seconds later, Mel was walking up an impossibly wide staircase with Ro. And she still hadn't had a chance to say more than a handful of words to her father.

"I gave you the spare bedroom with the street view," said Ro as they reached the top of the staircase. "But you're welcome to switch to another room if you'd like."

Ro headed about halfway down the hallway, opened a door, and ushered Mel into her room. Its color scheme was heavy on pastels, and its furniture looked like something out of a black-and-white movie. But it was huge and full of natural light. "There are some clothes in here that ought to fit you," Ro added, opening the closet. "I estimated your size based on the photos you sent Jasper. Bellamy's is a fairly formal restaurant, so I'd suggest wearing one of these to tea."

She plucked two outfits out of the closet and laid them on the bed. Both were businesslike suit-jacket and skirt combos. Plain design, expensive-looking fabric. This wasn't exactly evil stepmother treatment, but Mel still wasn't wildly enthused about the idea of Ro managing her wardrobe.

"Um, thanks," she said uneasily. "Will I get kicked out if I wear jeans?"

Ro laughed. She seemed to laugh a lot. "Nobody will kick you out if you're with us, but you might get some stares. Though, to be honest, you'll probably get the stares anyway. Most of the usuals at Bellamy's know our family and will be wondering about you."

"Oh," said Mel. "Great. Then I guess the jeans won't make a difference one way or the other, huh?"

"Well," Ro said carefully. "How you dress *will* influence the impression you make."

Mel glanced at herself in one of the room's roughly seven million mirrors. She looked a little more rumpled and tired than she normally did, but otherwise she looked like herself. An ordinary American teenager, not a member of a wealthy and ancient royal family. She imagined a bunch of snobby strangers looking at her, judging her, deciding that it had made perfect sense for Jasper Valmont to dump her mother. "Ah. Sure. Message received."

Ro's smile sprang back into action. "Wonderful. See you downstairs in a few minutes. If you need anything, just give a shout."

Mel thought briefly about all the things she needed. Time alone with her father. A chance to get her bearings in this strange house and this strange country. A breakfast burrito. "Thanks," she said to Ro. "I'm sure I'll be fine."

***

LaRue drove them all to the restaurant. It was only a five-minute drive, but it felt longer than the transatlantic flight. Ro did her best to get a conversation started, but Mel had trouble paying attention. She kept looking over at Jasper, waiting for him to say something. But he kept *not* saying something. Finally Mel resorted to pulling her phone out of the weird little handbag that came with her fancy outfit.

She messaged her friends: *Either Evonian fashion is a little wonky or everyone in this family dresses as if today's their day in court.*

At Bellamy's, a host instantly seated them. Their table was draped in a spotless white cloth and covered with a dizzying variety of silverware. A crystal chandelier hung overhead, and formally dressed waiters walked by carrying the kinds of dishes Mel had only seen on TV.

An awkward silence fell over the table while they all looked at their menus. Mel didn't recognize any of the dishes. Possibly because she didn't speak any French. When the waiter showed up, the Js both ordered their food in perfect French accents. When it was her turn, Mel said quickly, "The same for me," and hoped Jess hadn't ordered something completely inedible.

While they waited for their food to arrive, Mel glanced around, trying to figure out if anyone was staring at her. A lot of people were. *Good thing I'm not in jeans or somebody might've fainted.*

Ro said, "So, in terms of the week's schedule, Jasper has a board meeting this afternoon, I've got a couple of conference calls, and the girls have their piano lesson. But we'll all be free for supper, and then the rest of the week should be fairly relaxed until the party on Saturday."

"The party?" Mel asked.

Ro darted a concerned look at Jasper. "You did tell her about the party, Jasper, didn't you?"

"Erm—it—may have slipped my mind." Jasper gave his wife an apologetic look that he then turned to Mel. "My mother, Lady Cecily, is having a birthday party at my parents' estate. We're all going."

"Oh," said Mel. "Do your parents . . . want to meet me?" After all, these were the people who'd ruined his relationship with Mel's mom.

Jess chimed in. "No, but the whole family's invited, and Mum and Dad say you count as part of the family so you're going too."

Ro grimaced. "Jess," she said under her breath.

Mel looked over at her half sister. "Thank you for clearing that up." She had to admire the girl's bluntness, if nothing else.

Jess took a piece of candy out of her skirt pocket, unwrapped it, and popped into her mouth. Jasper sighed. "Jess, what did I tell you about eating those during mealtimes?"

"I'm not sure," said Jess, giving her father a wide-eyed innocent look. "I just remember you telling me to eat one if I thought I was about to say something rude."

At last, Jasper made an attempt to change the subject. Looking at Mel, he said, "I'll be attending an auction at Swithby's tomorrow morning."

"Sorry, Swith-who's?" said Mel.

"Swithby's is a fine art broker."

"Oh, okay. A what?"

"They sell valuable things," Jess jumped in, "like art and jewelry and antique clocks."

"Ah," said Mel. "Well, that's great."

"I was wondering if you'd like to come along," said Jasper. "The girls have their horseback riding lesson on Wednesday mornings, and Ro's meeting with some contractors about renovations to our house. So it would just be the two of us."

Mel tried not to show too much of a reaction to that last sentence. But on the inside, she was doing a victory dance. This would be a chance to hang out with her father one on one, without Family 2.0 hovering around them. "I think I can fit that into my schedule," she said brightly.

"Excellent," said Jasper, looking pleased. For the first time he seemed like the same person who'd answered her email with such a welcoming tone. "I'll be shopping around for some new paintings to add to the entryway after the renovations are done. I thought maybe you'd like to bid on something for yourself? So that you wouldn't be too bored."

"Uh, sure," said Mel, reaching for her water glass. "I didn't really set aside much of my budget for buying antiques, but if there's like a really tiny hairpin or something . . ."

"Oh, you don't have to use your own money," he said quickly. "Bid on whatever you like, and I'll pay for it—anything up to, say, two thousand euro."

Mel almost choked on her water. "Two *thousand* euro? Isn't the euro basically the same as the dollar?"

"It's worth a little more than the dollar at the moment actually," Joss piped up. *What are you doing with your life, kid?* Mel wondered.

"Well," she said to Jasper, "I really don't think that's necessary. I'm not gonna try to buy a summer home."

"Those are worth millions of euro," Joss informed her.

"Okay," said Mel flatly. *Evonians really do NOT get sarcasm, do they?* she thought.

"Don't worry about it," said Jasper. "I'm perfectly comfortable setting aside that amount. Spend as much or as little of it as you want."

"Are you trying to buy Mel's love, Dad?" asked Jess with a completely straight face.

"Of course not, sweetheart," Jasper replied—a little too quickly, Mel thought. But at the moment, she was in no mood to worry about that.

**4**

The next morning, Mel met Jasper in the front hall. "Hi," she said brightly. "Is it okay if I go dressed like this?" She gestured vaguely at her T-shirt and jeans. "Ro picked out some really nice clothes for me but they're not quite my size." This was actually a lie—Ro's estimates had been eerily accurate—but Jasper didn't need to know that.

"Oh, I'm sure that'll be fine," said Jasper in a tone that wasn't very convincing. "LaRue's waiting out front. Shall we?"

"Sure," said Mel.

Once they were in the car, Jasper asked, "So . . . how was your breakfast?"

*Talking about meals again*, thought Mel

with a sinking feeling in her stomach. "Very tasty. It was really nice of Baines to bring it up on a tray. I wasn't totally sure what flavor the jam was . . ."

"It was probably elderberry," said Jasper. "At least, that's what came with *my* toast this morning."

*I'm going to die of boredom before we even get to this auction*, thought Mel in despair. *Why can't he ask me something about myself? Like what I do for fun or who my friends are or what I think of my mom's new boyfriend . . . Would talking to What's His Name be this boring? Is Sir Jasper Valmont of the Evonian royal family more boring than WHAT'S HIS NAME? How can this be happening?!*

Mel flung herself into a last-ditch attempt at a real conversation. "So about this birthday party for your mom—what should I expect?"

"Ah, well, it'll be at my father's country house, about a half hour's drive from Alaborn. I expect it to be fairly elaborate. My parents have actually been on quite a tight budget for the past several years—"

"Really? I assumed you were all insanely rich." Quickly, Mel added, "Not that I care, just—aren't royal families usually rich?"

"You would think so," said Jasper. "But we live on a fixed income provided by the government, and some of us have spent it more wisely than others. Or married into richer noble families." *Ah*, thought Mel. *So Ro's family is rolling in money.* "My parents have been a little reckless with their money, I'm afraid. But they would never admit that to anyone outside the immediate family. They're going to put on a good show for my mother's party. Especially because my mother's brother died recently and my mother is becoming, er, more aware of her own mortality, I think."

"So it's gonna be an I'm-not-dead-ye' blowout?"

"Essentially. In a classy way."

"Sure." Mel and Jasper excha' little smile.

"And since the guest lis' you won't have to worry drawing too much att'

*p/*

*didn*

Mel's smile faltered. "Uh—it hadn't occurred to me to worry about that." Though after the Bellamy's outing, maybe it should've.

"I don't mean *negative* attention necessarily, it's just—there aren't that many members of the royal family who have illegitimate children."

"Illegitimate?" A surprised little snort escaped Mel's throat. "Why is that a big deal? People who aren't married have kids all the time."

"Not people like us."

*Right.*

"You see, everything we do is about carrying on the family line," said Jasper. "Preserving the family legacy. That's our job, our life's work. Anything that happens outside those lines is seen as . . . questionable. It's nothing personal against you—I want you to know that."

*Wow, thanks,* thought Mel dryly.

"It's just that the Valmont family prefers to play by its established rules."

Mel mulled this over for a minute. "So you didn't marry Ro for love?"

Jasper's eyes widened a little. "Of course I did. Ro is wonderful."

"But she was also somebody your parents signed off on?"

"Well, yes. The two things did line up like that."

"And what happens if they don't?"

Jasper was silent. But Mel already knew the answer.

*** 

Swithby's was basically a large room filled with rows of folding chairs and a podium at the front. When Mel and Jasper walked in, people were milling around and chatting, but hardly anyone had actually sat down yet. A woman greeted Jasper by name and handed him a stack of paper paddles with wooden handles.

"So you've never been to one of these, I take it?" Jasper asked Mel.

"Auctions for expensive old stuff? Nah, can't say it's really what the youth of America are into these days. How does this work?"

"Well, everyone gets these paddles—you hold up the appropriate paddle when you want to make a bid for something." He showed her how different numbers were printed on each paddle. "The auctioneer runs the event, so she'll start by showing off an item and explaining its background. Then she'll suggest a starting bid."

"And people bid until nobody wants to go any higher."

"Right. See, you'll catch on quickly."

Mel felt a little kick of pride in her chest. Even though this wasn't exactly rocket science, it was nice to know that Jasper—her *father*— had faith in her ability to keep up with what was happening.

Then, without warning, the color drained out of Jasper's face and his whole body went stiff. Mel followed his gaze and saw an older man walking toward them. The guy was probably in his late sixties and looked like he didn't work out much, but he was moving across the room pretty fast.

"Good morning, Jasper."

"Dad!" Jasper stuttered. It was extremely weird to hear such an informal word burst out of his mouth in that refined accent. "What, er, what brings you here?"

"Your mother sent me to take care of some business for her. And what about you?"

"Well, I just thought I'd pop by with . . ." Jasper turned to look at Mel as if he'd suddenly remembered she was there. "With Melissa. This is Melissa, by the way. She's my—that is—I've been telling you about her."

*Daughter*, Mel thought in a flash of irritation. *The word you're looking for is DAUGHTER. As in, yours. As in, this guy's granddaughter.*

"Mmmm, yes," said the older man dryly, looking at Mel as if she were a tough stain on a jacket.

So this was her grandfather—one half of the team that had split up her parents. Unlike Ro and the Js, he gave off exactly the kind of vibe she'd expected: hostile and smug.

"And of course, Melissa, this is my father, Sir Reginald Strathney," Jasper added unnecessarily. Mel wondered briefly why he was suddenly calling her by her full name. Maybe it was his way of reminding her to be polite. Well, she wasn't some little kid. She could act mature in front of a man who'd called her mom trash. They had no *idea* how mature she could be. She would boggle their minds with her maturity.

"Nice to meet you," Mel said to Sir Reginald, holding out her hand.

Sir Reginald ignored her outstretched hand. "Looks like her mother, doesn't she?"

Mel dropped her hand. "Not really," she said. *So much for acting mature.* "You can call me Mel, by the way."

"That won't be necessary," said Sir Reginald. "Jasper, I'll let you find a seat. We'll see you at the party."

"Right, yes, thank you, Dad," Jasper said quickly—but not quickly enough to finish before Sir Reginald had turned and walked away.

"Well, that was interesting," said Mel, proud of herself for keeping her tone neutral.

"Let's just sit down," said Jasper. He sounded exhausted. On one level Mel felt sorry for him. Interacting with his dad had obviously stressed him out. On another level . . . *Dude, you couldn't even call me your daughter in front of that jerk?*

\*\*\*

From Mel's point of view, the auction did not get off to a promising start. Lot One, the first item up for sale, was a collection of eighteenth-century china dishes. Somebody eventually bid twelve thousand euro on it. Next came an early twentieth-century landscape painting that showed what Alaborn had looked like a hundred years ago. Jasper bought it for nine hundred euro. Then there was a set of super old decorative hair combs that looked like gaudy seashells. Mel was starting to wonder how she would break it to Jasper that nothing here was interesting enough for her to bid on.

"And now for Lot Thirteen," announced the auctioneer. "The complete correspondence between Lord Maximilian Valmont, the Duke of Rotherham, and Miss Beatrice Allard."

"Ohhhh no," said Jasper in a strangled whisper.

"What?" Mel asked him. "Who's Maximilian Valmont?"

"My grandfather," replied Jasper in the same mortified voice.

With her gloved hands, the auctioneer gently picked up a packet of papers tied together with twine. Mel glanced at Jasper again. "Are those letters?"

"Erm," said Jasper—half stutter, half gulp.

"The letters," the auctioneer went on, "were written between 1942 and 1957 and were recently rediscovered by the Allard family. They are rumored to be of an amorous nature . . ."

Mel sat bolt upright in her chair. "They're *love* letters?"

Her voice came out a little more loudly than she'd intended. It was still technically a whisper, but it carried through the whole room. Several people turned to glance in her direction. Jasper's eyes widened with alarm.

"Sorry," she mouthed at him.

The auctioneer cleared her throat and continued. "The Duke of Rotherham, the favorite brother of Her Royal Highness Queen Emilia the First, carried on a love affair with Miss Allard for several years before marrying Lady Anne Irvine. They continued to correspond by letter for several years *after* that. This collection has been in the possession of Miss Allard's family for the past several decades. The owners are now asking for a starting bid of five hundred euro."

Mel's eyes were now glued to the stack of papers the auctioneer was holding. Love letters between her royal great-grandfather and an ordinary woman like her mom.

Someone raised a paddle.

Wait—not just someone. She recognized the man. It was Sir Reginald.

"Very good," said the auctioneer, nodding at Mel's grandfather. "Do I see six hundred?"

Mel raised her paddle.

The auctioneer pointed to her. "Six hundred, do I see seven hundred?"

Sir Reginald held up his paddle again without looking her way.

"Seven hundred," the auctioneer confirmed, pointing to Mel's grandfather. "Do I see . . ."

Mel's arm shot into the air before he had even said "Eight hundred."

This time, Sir Reginald turned to see who was bidding against him. And when he saw Mel holding up her paddle, his eyes bulged. So did a vein in his neck. Mel raised her eyebrows at him. *Oh, I'm so sorry, did you want these letters? Whoops.*

Beside her, Jasper coughed nervously. "Mel, are you certain this is what you want?"

Mel flashed him her most innocent smile. "Definitely."

The auctioneer was still trying to drive up the price. Sir Reginald bid nine hundred, then Mel bid again, and back and forth and back and forth until—

"Two thousand from Sir Reginald," the auctioneer announced.

Crap. That was her limit.

"Do I hear two thousand one-hundred?"

Mel didn't move. Her grandfather shot her a look of cold triumph.

"Going once," said the auctioneer. "Going twice . . ."

Mel raised her paddle again.

She ignored Jasper's cough, which sounded a little more urgent this time.

"Twenty one hun—twenty *two* hundred," said the auctioneer, tripping over herself as Sir Reginald outbid Mel yet again.

This was going to drag on for years at this rate. Before she could stop herself, Mel blurted out, "Three thousand!"

A collective gasp filled the room, as if the walls themselves were sucking in their breath.

"Ahhhh," stammered the auctioneer. "Three thousand euro. Going once . . . going twice . . . *sold* to the young lady in the green shirt!"

Mel glanced down at her shirt to confirm its color. Yep, green. She'd won.

When the auction ended, Jasper hastily
signed some paperwork and arranged for
their winnings to be delivered to Darnley
Place later that day. While he was doing
that, several people walked up to Mel and
introduced themselves. They all seemed to
know who she was—and they all seemed to
want something.

One guy said he ran a fashion line and
asked if she was interested in modeling. Before
she could even answer, he gave her his card,
saying, "One of the LePointe girls models for
us, you know, and a couple of the Fontaines.
But we'd love to have someone from the actual
*royal* family in our ranks."

One lady in charge of some charity foundation wondered if she would like to make a donation. Mel stammered out something polite about having to check with her dad first.

And then there was the guy who owned a newspaper. "I would be very interested in interviewing you for the *Alaborn Star*, Miss Novak. Just an informal conversation. A newcomer's perspective on the inner workings of the royal family. I'd also be interested in taking a look at those letters you've just bought, if you'd be willing to arrange that . . ."

At this point, Jasper was finally done with the paperwork. "If you're looking for your next front-page story, I suggest you look elsewhere," he said to the newspaper owner with surprising firmness. Then he turned to Mel.

"Let's get out of here . . ."

But then Sir Reginald's voice boomed out behind them. "Jasper! May I have a word?"

Jasper and Mel both turned to see Sir Reginald glowering at them.

"Yes, Dad?" Jasper said, his voice cracking with nervousness. The confidence he'd shown when he brushed off the newspaper owner vanished instantly.

"I'm sure it won't come as a surprise to you, Jasper, that your grandmother sent me here specifically to buy those letters. I'd appreciate it if you would turn them over to me now."

"Uh, sorry, did I miss something?" said Mel. "Last time I checked, *I* bought the letters."

Sir Reginald ignored her. "They belong in our family vault, Jasper. They're your grandfather's private correspondence. Your mother would be mortified if her father's personal life was splashed all over the tabloids."

"Who said anything about tabloids?" Mel blurted out. "These people have been dead for ages, haven't they? Why would gossip columnists care about their letters?"

Sir Reginald gave her a stony look. "Young lady, clearly you don't understand the stature of the royal family. My wife's father was not merely the Duke of Rotherham. He was a prince—the son of a king, and the brother of a queen. His life may be over, but it will *always* matter to the citizens of this country."

Mel fought the urge to roll her eyes.

Sir Reginald turned back to Jasper. "It is crucial that those letters be kept out of public view, Jasper. To preserve your grandfather's reputation and your mother's peace of mind."

"But—" Mel started to protest.

Sir Reginald cut her off. "This is absolutely none of your business, young lady. It is no one's business."

"Except yours and your wife's? I'm not following your logic here."

"Erm . . ." said Jasper.

"I'm not gonna sell these letters to a tabloid, if that's what you're worried about," Mel went on. "I'm not gonna post excerpts on my social media. I just bought them because I'd like to have them—the same way Jasper bought that painting."

Sir Reginald aimed a shocked look at Jasper. "She calls you *Jasper*?"

Was there anything that didn't scandalize this guy? "You're gonna have to excuse us," before he got married. And then he stayed in touch with her after he was married. That's kinda shady and not really fair to his wife, I guess, but it's not like he was a serial killer or something."

Jasper shook his head in exasperation. "It's the fact that the woman he was involved with was Beatrice Allard, a well-known anti-monarchist journalist."

"Is that supposed to clear things up for me?" asked Mel.

Jasper blinked at her a few times. "You do know that until fairly recently, Evonia was an absolute monarchy, with the ruler making all the governing decisions for the nation?"

"Uh, sure."

"Well, Allard was one of the people who spoke out against that, especially in the articles she wrote. She believed the government should transition into a constitutional monarchy."

"Meaning—"

"Meaning that instead of the king or queen making the laws, the government would be run by elected officials. She played a huge

"Why? It's not like she's that high in the line of succession, right? She never would've had a shot at becoming queen or anything."

"Of course not. We're miles away from inheriting the crown."

"Then why should it matter to her that the queen doesn't have any real power?"

Jasper sighed and shrugged. "She likes knowing she belongs at the top of an ancient social order. She'd prefer for the nation to be controlled by her relatives, not by strangers she's never heard of who chose to put their names on a ballot."

"So you're saying she's a control freak."

"That's a crude way of putting it."

"But accurate?"

"Fairly." Jasper let out a resigned sigh.

Mel desperately wanted to ask if this was why Lady Cecily had made Jasper break up with Mel's mom. But she was afraid that would make Jasper uncomfortable again, right when he finally seemed to be opening up to her. The last thing she wanted was to ruin this moment—it may be the weirdest case of family bonding ever, but she would take what she could get.

***

They actually did meet Ro and the Js for lunch. Bellamy's again. Mel was starting to wonder if this family had heard of any other restaurants.

"How was the auction?" Ro asked as Mel and Jasper joined her and the girls at the same table they'd sat at yesterday.

"We ran into Sir Reginald," Mel said, "and I bought some old letters that my great-grandfather wrote to a lady he didn't marry, and Sir Reginald had a tantrum about it."

Ro's hand flew to her mouth. "Heavens, the Allard letters?"

"Yep," said Mel.

Ro looked from Mel to Jasper and back to Mel. Then she burst out laughing.

"It wasn't amusing," muttered Jasper, still looking mortified.

"It kinda was," said Mel, shrugging.

"Well, congratulations, Mel," said Ro. "If you'd like to get a better look at the letters, I can get you some gloves and the right kind of lighting . . ."

"I—sorry—gloves?" Mel said in confusion.

"You'll want to avoid damaging them."

Mel flushed. "I'll be careful with them."

"Oh, of course you will!" Ro said hastily. "It's just that with any older document that has historic significance, it's important to do everything possible to preserve it. You don't want the natural oils from your hands seeping into the paper, or . . ."

"Ohhh," said Mel, relieved that Ro hadn't thought she was going to fold the letters into paper airplanes or something.

"I used to work in the archives at the National Museum," Ro added. "So this is the sort of thing I'm trained to do."

"Well then, sure, I'd love your help," said Mel, even though she couldn't quite believe she'd just agreed to spend even more time with her stepmother.

"How was the riding lesson, girls?" Jasper asked the Js. And just like that, the focus shifted away from Mel. As she watched him listen to his other daughters summarize their interactions with horses named Prudence and Delilah, Mel couldn't help feeling jealous and a little confused. Jasper clearly knew how to act like a normal dad—asking questions, listening, even laughing when his kids said something clever or funny. Why didn't he act like that with her? Why had they only talked about elderberry jam and the reputations of dead people?

After a while Jasper's phone started buzzing. "Sorry, I'd better take this," he muttered. "It's the queen's social secretary—probably calling about Mother's birthday gift."

As soon as he stepped away from the table, Joss looked at Mel. *What insult is she about to drop on me now?* Mel wondered.

"So when you say Grandfather had a tantrum," Joss asked, "did his face get splotchy, or did he just give you the death glare?"

Feeling a mixture of shock and amusement, Mel replied, "Just the death glare. What does it take to make him splotchy-faced?"

"Joss," said Ro sternly, "there's no need to speak ill of your grandfather."

"He got splotchy-faced when Dad told him about you," Jess piped up, speaking to Mel. "He told Dad that since you were illegitimate you wouldn't ever be able to inherit his title and that you and your mum were probably just trying to get your hands on the family money. Even though we don't actually have *that* much money anymore."

Joss opened her mouth to add something— probably her best guess at how much money was in her father's bank account, knowing this kid. But Ro cut her off. "That's enough, both of you. It's very rude of you to say that sort of thing in front of Mel."

"It was Grandfather who said it," Jess protested. "We just repeated it."

Mel jumped in. "Actually, I don't mind—I appreciate that they're being so honest with me." She glanced at Ro. "And for the record, I'm not after anybody's money, and neither is my mom."

"We guessed that," said Joss. "Because if you were, you'd probably be a lot more careful around Grandfather."

It occurred to Mel that her half sisters weren't trying to give her a hard time. They actually looked impressed with her. Speaking their minds might even be their way of showing they liked her. She would have to get used to that.

**6**

That afternoon, Jasper had another board meeting for a charity organization he sponsored, so Mel ended up taking her letters—which had arrived shortly after lunch in what looked like an old shoebox—to Ro's private study. It was a surprisingly comfortable-looking room full of stacks of books and papers and notebooks. And surprisingly *messy*.

As she'd promised, Ro supplied Mel with a pair of cloth gloves and sat her down under a lamp that gave off very gentle light. "I can leave you alone if you'd like," she added as Mel took the lid off the shoebox.

"Uh, actually—I think I might have trouble reading their handwriting," Mel confessed. "Do you think you could stay and help with that?"

Ro beamed at her, as if this was the greatest honor she could imagine. "I'd be happy to!"

So for the next three hours, Mel and Ro went through a portion of the 871 letters written by Lord Maximilian and Beatrice Allard. Mel got into the habit of reading them out loud, with Ro looking over her shoulder and following along. Whenever Mel got to a word or phrase she couldn't make out, Ro helped.

"I really like Beatrice," Mel commented. "I mean, her voice in these letters is so sassy."

"I met her once," said Ro. "She gave a lecture at my school. She seemed marvelous. And of course I knew Lord Maximilian, though not very well. He'd passed away by the time I married into the Valmont family."

"But you're from some fancy noble family too, right?" Mel asked. "So you would've hung out with the Valmonts even before you and Jasper got together?"

"We moved in the same circles, yes," said Ro. Then, to Mel's surprise, she rolled her eyes. "Not that my background helped win over Sir Reginald and Lady Cecily."

"Really?" said Mel. "I would have thought you'd be their idea of a perfect daughter-in-law."

"Well, I certainly did my best. I gave up my job when I married Jasper so that I could 'focus on the family.' And I let a lot of old friendships fizzle because those friends weren't the kind of people Sir Reginald and Lady Cecily respected. I went through all the motions, but nothing has ever been enough for them."

"That sucks. I'm sorry," said Mel, and to her own surprise, she meant it.

Ro's smile looked a little forced. "It's not all bad, though! I did snag an amazing husband and ended up with two delightful daughters. Three, actually, if you don't mind me counting you."

Mel let that sink in. A few days ago she would've assumed Ro was being fake, trying to gain her trust just so that she could stab Mel in the back later. But now that felt ridiculous.

She wasn't sure she was totally comfortable with Ro claiming her as a daughter, but she couldn't deny that Ro was being genuinely kind. She found herself returning her stepmother's smile.

7

"So how's it going?" asked Mel's mom. Her face blurred and flickered across Mel's laptop screen, and her voice sounded far away. Which, of course, it was.

"Not bad," said Mel. "The butler brings me breakfast every morning, which was weird at first, but now I kind of love it. And then Ro plans these outings for us during the day. We went to a museum on Thursday, and yesterday we drove out into the countryside and had a picnic. I mean, LaRue drove us out into the countryside. It's weird that they have so many people working for them, but I guess that's normal for rich people in any country, right? And we have lunch or tea at the same ridiculous restaurant every day, which I don't get, but that might also be a rich people thing. And the food *is* good, so I guess I shouldn't complain. How are you?"

"Fine," said Mel's mom. "Todd and I are going to a movie tonight. I was actually thinking that when you get back, maybe the three of us could go see that new superhero movie . . ."

This again. Mel decided to wrap things up. "Mom, can I call you back later? There's this party tonight and I need to get ready for it." The party started at 7:00 p.m. and it was currently 10:00 a.m., but her mom didn't need to know that. Mel was actually planning to spend rest of the morning reading through Max and Beatrice's letters with Ro, but she figured her mom didn't need to know that either. She'd avoided telling her mom how much time she'd been spending with Ro. Especially because it probably added up to more time than she'd spent with Jasper—who was the whole reason she'd come here in the first place.

"Oh, sure, honey," said her mom. "We'll talk more soon. Have a great time!"

Mel sighed as she ended the call. Her mom was trying really hard to be supportive. But it was so obvious that the kind of life Jasper and Ro had was completely unappealing to her mom. She clearly didn't feel that Mel had been missing out on anything all these years. Mel couldn't help disagreeing. Being here was strange, but she wouldn't trade it for an outing to the movies with her mom and What's His Name.

Ro was waiting for Mel in the study. They were almost done going through the letters—they only had a few left. Mel found herself wishing there were more. It had been strangely fun to spend the last few mornings hunched over almost-unreadable handwriting, reading the jokes and secrets and radical ideas of these two people she'd never meet.

The last few letters also turned out to be the saddest. Max was married and had two kids, and he was finally ending the correspondence since he knew it could hurt his family. He and Beatrice said some very touching things, and then some very matter-of-fact things, and then it was game over as they both decided to move on with separate lives.

"That's so sad," said Mel as they finished reading the last letter.

"In a way," Ro agreed. "But it's also rather lovely, don't you think?"

Mel didn't think so at all, but she didn't want to burst Ro's bubble, so she kept quiet.

"So," sighed Ro, standing up and stretching. "What do you think you'd like to do with these letters now? You have every right to keep them to yourself, of course. But you could also donate them to the National Museum if you want. They definitely have historical significance."

Mel looked up in surprise. "Lady Cecily would hate that."

"Yes," said Ro with a straight face. "She absolutely would."

Mel grinned at her.

8

Mel wandered around Darnley Place by herself that afternoon. Ro had to rush off to yet another meeting with contractors for the upcoming home renovations, and Jasper was MIA again. Eventually Mel made her way into the sitting room, the first room of the house that she'd seen when she arrived.

The Js were in there, with that same board game sprawled out on the floor. "You need to roll twenty or higher to avoid the burns," Joss was saying to Jess was Mel walked in.

Then they both looked up at her as if she were some sort of alien.

"Sorry to bother you," said Mel. "Your mom said there was a coffee table book about the National Museum in here. I just came by to grab it."

"That sounds incredibly boring," said Joss.

"Yeah, well, you're the one who keeps track of the strength of the euro compared to the dollar," Mel retorted before she could stop herself. "And didn't you have a *tennis* lesson yesterday?"

"Our grandparents insist on that sort of thing," said Joss. "We both hate tennis."

"We like riding, though," added Jess. "Do you like riding?"

"Sure, in theory," said Mel, glancing around for the book Ro had described to her.

"It's easy to like something in theory," said Jess. "I like our grandparents in theory, for example."

Mel paused. "Oh? You only like them in theory? Not in real life?"

"Grandmother's a *nightmare*," said Joss, rolling her eyes. "Every time she sees me she criticizes what I'm wearing and my hair and my pimples and my teeth and—ugh! It's exhausting."

"And Grandfather just sort of looks at us," added Jess, "like he can't quite decide whether he'll admit he knows us."

"Oh, I thought that was a special reaction just for me."

"Sorry to disappoint you," said Joss wryly. "He and Grandmother are critical of *everybody*."

"That's actually kind of reassuring." Mel started to head for a bookcase and ended up accidently kicking over a stack of tokens on the floor. "Whoops, sorry. What *is* this game you two are always playing?"

"Dragon Empire," said Jess. "Want to play with us? We can start over."

Mel looked at the board skeptically. "What are the rules?"

Jess sat up straighter. "You're a dragon and you're trying to take over as many countries as possible. You get seven skill cards, twenty resource tokens, three one-time-use special powers . . ."

Five hours later, Jess won the game and Joss declared that they should start getting ready for the party.

"Did Mum pick out an outfit for you?" asked Jess as they all headed upstairs.

"Yeah, she gave me a couple options to choose from," said Mel. "Does she do that for you too?"

"Only for formal occasions," said Jess, pulling a handful of little candies out of her pocket. She held one out to Mel. "Have you ever had one of these?"

"Don't think so," said Mel, squinting at the unfamiliar wrapper.

"It's called an *éclat*—that's a French word that basically means a burst or explosion, which is what they do in your mouth. They're only made in Evonia."

Mel popped one into her mouth and bit into it. A flash of fizzy bittersweetness filled her mouth. "This is amazing. Do you have more?"

"I do, but how much are they worth to you?" said Jess. "Shall we start the bidding at, say, three thousand euro?"

Mel laughed. "How about I just trade you my antique letters for your bag of candy?"

"If only Grandfather knew it could be so easy!"

Mel snorted with laughter. She was actually starting to like these girls.

*   *   *

Mel had just finished getting ready when there was a knock on her door. "Come on in, Baines!" she called, assuming it was the butler.

Instead, Jasper poked his head in. "Thought I'd, er, see how you were doing."

*How unusual for you to bother asking.* The thought flashed through her mind, but instead she said lightly, "Trying to decide which shoes will be the least uncomfortable. Doesn't anyone in Evonian wear flats?"

"Ordinary people probably do," said Jasper with a sheepish shrug.

Mel sighed, kicked off the shoes she'd been trying on, and sat down cross-legged on the floor. "Give me some tips on surviving a party hosted by non-ordinary Evonians," she said to Jasper. "What should I expect? How should I act?"

"Hmm," said Jasper, frowning thoughtfully as he sat down in a straight-backed chair. "It's probably best to call my mother 'my lady' and my father 'Sir Reginald,' unless they invite you to be more informal with them. They still prefer for Ro to call them by their titles even after all this time."

Mel gave him a stunned look, but Jasper just plowed on. "And if anyone talks to you in French, just smile and say *'je ne parle pas le français.'* Don't ask 'What?' or anything vulgar like that."

"Wouldn't dream of being vulgar," said Mel, popping another exploding candy into her mouth.

Jasper saw it and made a comical grimace. "Don't tell me you've gotten addicted to those too."

"Guess it runs in the family."

At that, Jasper smiled, reached into his pocket, and pulled out an éclat of his own. "You may be right."

9

The car ride to Sir Reginald's summer house was actually very pleasant. Joss played snippets of Evonian pop songs on her phone and made Mel try to guess the rest of the lyrics. Jasper even joined in, making terrible guesses. All five of them were laughing by the time they reached the estate.

But as soon as LaRue dropped them off at the front door, things got weird.

The house was even bigger and grander than Darnley Place. The butler who met them in the front hall was a lot more elaborately dressed than Baines. "Sir Reginald and Lady Cecily have not come down yet, sir," he informed Jasper. "But the guests have gathered in the library, the parlor, and the ballroom."

"I feel like someone's gonna get murdered any second," Mel muttered to the Js as they entered what must be the ballroom. When they gave her blank looks, she said, "You know, Colonel So-and-So in the ballroom with the wrench? Don't you have that game in Evonia?"

"No," said Jess. "You'll have to teach us how it works."

Mel smiled. "Deal."

People in formal attire were milling around while equally formally dressed staff offered them refreshments on silver trays. Mel didn't recognize most of the appetizers, but they looked very elaborate and seafoody. She remembered what Jasper had said about his parents being on a tighter budget than they liked to admit. From the looks of those appetizers, their credit card debt had probably spiked recently.

The people at the party all seemed to know Jasper and Ro and the Js. A lot of them said "And who's this?" in a tone of fake enthusiasm and curiosity—which made it clear they knew exactly who Mel was. Jasper kept introducing her as Melissa Novak-Valmont, which was way too many syllables for her liking.

A few people actually seemed friendly and even interesting. Mel was in the middle of a surprisingly enjoyable exchange with Jasper's cousin Louisa when everyone turned toward the French doors that bordered one side of the ballroom. Sir Reginald and a woman who must be Lady Cecily had just entered through those doors.

"Good evening," said the woman crisply, speaking to the room at large. "I hope you'll forgive my late entrance. Sir Reginald and I have just been taking a stroll in the garden. Thank you all for coming."

The whole crowd replied with vague, respectful-sounding murmurs, and people raised their wine glasses in Lady Cecily's general direction. Cousin Louisa smiled at Mel and her family. "I'd better let you say hello."

"Right," said Jasper, squaring his shoulders. He led Ro, Mel, and the Js over to his parents.

"Hello, Mother." Jasper gave her a quick, awkward peck on the cheek. "Happy birthday."

"Hard to be happy about turning sixty-five," said Lady Cecily. "But I suppose we have to make the best of things. Speaking of making the best of things, Rosalie, did you wear that same dress to my niece's charity fundraiser?"

"I'm sure you're thinking of another dress, my lady," said Ro with an innocent smile. "I do tend to stick to the same color palette. Happy birthday."

"Happy birthday, Grandmother," chimed the Js in eerie unison. Mel had to stifle a laugh at how well they pulled it off.

"I'm glad to see you girls have made yourselves presentable for once," was Lady Cecily's response.

Jasper cleared his throat. "Mother, this is Melissa. Melissa, Lady Cecily Valmont."

*Deploying the charming smile.* "Pleasure to finally meet you, my lady. And happy birthday."

"Have you got anything original to say, Miss Nomak?" said Lady Cecily dryly.

Mel kept smiling through gritted teeth. "It's Novak," she corrected her grandmother. "Is *that* original enough for you, my lady?"

Lady Cecily blinked once, very slowly, as if blinking a second time would be beneath her. "I understand that you're the person who's currently in possession of my father's personal correspondence."

"Yep," Mel chirped.

"And do you really think you're the best person to keep those letters?"

"Probably not. I'm actually thinking of donating them to the National Museum."

Lady Cecily's whole face froze, except for her eyes, which were horrified and angry. "You can't be serious."

"I would never lie about something so important," said Mel sweetly.

"Anyway," Jasper cut in, shooting a nervous glance in Mel's direction, "Melissa will be here for another few weeks, Mother, so you'll have plenty of time to see more of her. Right now we won't keep you from the rest of your guests . . ."

He put a hand on Mel's elbow and started steering her off to the side. Ro and the girls were already heading toward the nearest appetizer tray.

*Not a bad performance*, Mel thought. *I was polite, I kept my cool, I didn't let her get under my skin, and now I'm walking away calmly . . .*

"I don't know what I expected," Lady Cecily muttered to her husband. "Considering who her mother is."

*Scratch that.*

Mel spun around. "Excuse me?"

Lady Cecily stared back at her coldly. "I wasn't speaking to you, Miss Nolak."

"*Novak*. It's *Novak*. It's not that hard to remember. You have a gigantic family tree and everyone on it has fourteen different titles, and you're telling me you can't remember N-o-*v*-a-k?"

Mel didn't think she'd been talking that loudly, but the whole room had suddenly gone silent. Her voice echoed ten times more powerfully than it had at the auction.

And she didn't care.

"Young lady," said Lady Cecily, "you are out of line."

"No, *you* are out of line," Mel snapped. "What did you just say about my mother?"

"Only that it's not surprising that someone like her would raise such a disrespectful daughter."

"Someone like her? You mean caring and fun and down to earth?"

"I mean irresponsible and self-centered and vulgar," Lady Cecily snapped back. *Wow, the word vulgar really gets used a lot in this country.*

"It's interesting that you think you know so much about my mother, Lady Cecily. Considering that you've never met her."

"I know what kind of life she led and what kind of choices she made."

"Well, you don't get to judge her. You can *think* whatever you want about her, but you don't get to talk about her like that. Her choices are *none of your business*. I know that's a hard concept to grasp—that not everything revolves around you—but just trust me on this, okay? My mom has stayed out of your lives, just like you wanted. So you need to stay out of hers."

At this point, Jasper tried to take hold of Mel's elbow again. "Mel, if you could just—"

Mel jerked her arm away. "You know what, Jasper? I'm not the only one who feels this way. I'm not the only one you've thrown under the bus because you can't stand up to these people. It's one thing that you haven't been there for me—and that you ditched my mom the way you did. But you also let your wife and *legitimate* daughters get treated like crap. They're the people who are *supposed* to matter to you, and you can't even stand up for *them*. Is that a family tradition too?"

One look at Jasper's stunned expression made it clear that Mel wasn't going to get an answer. Ordinarily, she'd be proud of herself for delivering a zinger that had struck someone speechless. But right now, Jasper's silence was the last thing Mel wanted.

*Of course he isn't going to say anything,* she thought miserably. *Of course he isn't going to prove me wrong.*

So she played the last card she had, which was to storm dramatically out of the house through the French doors.

**10**

She only got as far as the garden. Then it hit her that she didn't know how to find the main entrance from here. And there was no way she could go back into the house now. Still fuming, Mel marched over to an elegant gazebo with white pillars and a little marble bench.

She sat down, pulled her phone out of her tiny handbag, and fired off a message to Elise and Savannah: *Just did some major bridge-burning with Jasper. I think I finally get why my mom reacted to the breakup the way she did. This dude is ridiculous. All he really cares about is not rocking the boat.*

Figuring she wouldn't get an immediate response, she put the phone away again. Maybe she could wait here until, say, four in the morning, and then sneak out once the other guests had left, while her grandparents and the staff were asleep. There were certainly less pleasant places to hide out. Not that this hard marble bench was all that comfortable, but still . . .

"Mel?" Mel thought about running for cover behind one of the hedges, but then she realized it was just Joss calling her name.

Joss came up the garden path to the gazebo with Jess trailing behind her. They grinned when they saw Mel.

"Hey, Js. How was that for a dramatic exit?" Mel asked them as they ran over to join her.

"It was *amazing*!" crowed Joss. "You left them completely speechless! I've never seen anyone have that effect on Grandmother and Grandfather."

"I kind of unloaded on your dad too," Mel pointed out.

"Dad deserved it," said Jess firmly. "He knows they're bullies and he never does anything about it."

"Yeah, but now I'm stuck at their house and I don't really know what to do," Mel sighed. "I can't exactly go back in there."

"I think I know where the car is parked," said Joss. "What if we just take Mum and Dad's car home?"

"Uh, how will *they* get home then?"

"LaRue can come back for them after he drops us off."

"This doesn't seem like a great strategy for making anyone less angry at me."

"No, but it'd be fun, wouldn't it?" said Jess.

Mel realized she was grinning. "You know what? Sure. Let's do it."

***

When Mel and the Js tapped on the front window of Jasper's car and asked LaRue to take them back to Darnley Place, the driver didn't question them. He just silently drove them home, with his weird Evonian pop station playing softly in the background.

Back at the house in Alaborn, the girls all went to their bedrooms. Mel flopped down on her bed and looked at her phone. Her friends had messaged her back, saying supportively insulting things about Jasper. Her mom had emailed her too: *Sorry we didn't get to talk for very long earlier. Hope you have a wonderful time at the party . . .*

Tears suddenly stung Mel's eyes, and she regretted how distant she had been to her mom. She still didn't think her mom had made the right decisions to keep the truth from her, but she'd done what she thought was best. She'd tried to support Mel even when it wasn't easy.

And, in Mel's mom's defense, what had Jasper done since he'd known about her? Paid for a plane ticket and a shopping spree. Called her Melissa Novak-Valmont as if a hyphenated name somehow made up for what he *wasn't* saying.

He had every right to be angry with her for ruining the party, but she was going to be angry right back.

Before she fell asleep she answered her mom's email: *Thanks for talking earlier. And by the way, it would be great to meet Todd when*

*I get home. As long as we don't have to go to a superhero movie, I'm in.*

***

Baines knocked on Mel's door earlier than usual. As Mel sat up in bed and peered at him through bleary eyes, she realized he wasn't carrying a breakfast tray. "Miss, your presence is requested downstairs in the breakfast room."

"Uh, right now?"

"Ideally, yes, miss."

"Okay. Where's the breakfast room?"

"Just off the main dining room, miss."

"Ah, right. Obviously. Thanks, Baines."

Mel threw on some jeans and a tank top and made her way downstairs. In the "breakfast room"—a small room with curved walls and a lot of windows—Jasper, Ro, and the Js were all sitting at a small round table eating flaky pastries.

Jasper looked up when she came in. "Ah. Mel. Good morning."

"Hey, everybody." Mel slid into the

empty chair at the table, between Jess and her stepmother.

"Morning!" chirped Jess and Joss. Ro gave Mel a small smile. Mel hoped that was a sign that she wasn't about to get kicked out of Darnley Place.

Jasper cleared his throat. "About the party last night—"

At that moment, Baines walked in. "Sir, Lady Cecily Valmont and Sir Reginald Strathney are here."

Mel bit back a groan. Couldn't they have waited to show up until she'd at least had a chance to eat breakfast?

"Thank you, Baines, send them in," said Jasper. Mel might've been imagining it, but she thought he looked distinctly less terrified than he usually did when his parents were around.

Sir Reginald and Lady Cecily almost knocked Baines over as they stormed into the room. "Hello, Dad, Mother," said Jasper calmly. "I'm glad you're here. I'm sure Mel will be very happy to accept your apology for what happened last night."

Mel turned to look at Jasper in amazement. *Was he actually standing up to his parents? For her?* She turned to look at Sir Reginald and Lady Cecily. They also seemed shaken by this turn of events, but their silent shock only lasted a few seconds.

"*Our* apology?" snapped lady Cecily. "If anyone should be apologizing—"

"But that's not why we're here," Sir Reginald cut her off. "We're here about the letters, Jasper. We would appreciate it if you returned them to your mother immediately."

Jasper set down the knife he'd been using to spread jam on his breakfast pastry. "Well, that's not up to me. It's up to Mel."

Lady Cecily bristled. "Those letters belong to our family."

"And they're staying in our family. Or are you telling me that my daughter doesn't count as family?"

There it was, finally. He'd said it—*my daughter.*

Lady Cecily sniffed and gave a dismissive little shrug. "Well, after all, Jasper, you haven't had a paternity test. For all we know, she's not your daughter at all!"

Mel saw Jasper's jaw clench. "Don't be ridiculous, Mother," he said in a very slow, deliberate voice. "Everyone can see that Mel's the spitting image of me. And I'm going to have to insist that you *never* question that again."

Lady Cecily's eyes widened ever so slightly. Mel had a feeling that Jasper had never used that tone with her before. Still, she clearly wasn't ready to let go of her main goal. "Your relationship with this girl is your own business, Jasper. I certainly have no interest in getting involved. But I must have those letters back."

"Fine," said Jasper, and Mel's heart dropped. But then he added, "Feel free to buy them from her. She paid three thousand euro for them. If you can top that, perhaps she'll consider selling them to you."

Sir Reginald gaped at his son. "This is outrageous! You know very well that our resources aren't what they used to be. You can't expect us to shell out money we can't spare, just to pay off our own—"

He broke off, but Jasper finished the sentence for him. "What? Your own *family*?"

Sir Reginald's expression turned to a glare. Lady Cecily was now visibly shaking with anger.

"Well," Jasper said calmly, "I suggest you give that some careful thought. In any case, it's up to Mel whether she decides to sell those letters. She has every right to refuse any offer you make and keep them for herself. Now should I have Baines show you out, or can you find the door on your own?"

"This is a disgraceful way to treat your parents, Jasper," Sir Reginald fumed.

"Probably," said Jasper. "I'll let you know if I'm struck with remorse at some point. Meanwhile, enjoy your day."

11

"That was pretty epic," Mel admitted after her grandparents had left in a huff. "Thanks so much, Jasper."

Jasper opened his mouth to say something, but Mel cut him off. "And now I think I'll go have another look at those famous letters. See you later, everyone."

She grabbed a roll from the table and booked it out of the room before anyone could protest. Jasper had done an excellent job of defending her just now, but that didn't change what had happened last night. Mel knew they still had an awkward conversation in their future. She just wasn't quite ready to deal with it yet.

She hunkered down in Ro's study, paging through Max and Beatrice's letters again.

After about an hour, Ro came in. "Still thinking about what to do with those?"

"Oh, I'm definitely giving them to the museum," said Mel. "If that sends Lady Cecily into a fainting fit, that's *her* problem, not mine."

Ro half laughed, half sighed. "I'm sure you're not in the mood to feel sorry for your grandmother, but . . . I do have some sympathy for her. I think I understand why the thought of those letters getting out is so painful to her."

"Because she hates true love?" Mel guessed.

Ro sighed. "Well, imagine how hard it must be for her to find out that her father loved a woman other than her mother his whole life. That her mother was his second choice. And that *she* was simply the living proof that he had done his duty and given up the life he *really* wanted."

"That would kind of suck," Mel admitted, feeling a little sorry for Lady Cecily in spite of herself. "But that's no excuse for her to treat other people so badly."

"I agree," said Ro. "And I wish there was a chance she might change her ways. But . . ."

"Don't worry," said Mel, "I won't hold my breath."

Looking down at the letters, she sighed. "I don't know. I'll give it some more thought. I still don't think I owe Lady Cecily anything—"

"I agree," said Ro.

"But when you really boil it down, these letters *are* private. I probably wouldn't be thrilled if my dad's letters to my mom got put on public display. I want to respect Max and Beatrice, you know?"

Ro nodded at this. "I understand completely."

"Especially since . . ." Mel shrugged, embarrassed. "Since they didn't exactly get a happy ending."

Ro took Mel's hand and gave it a little squeeze. "I do think they both found happiness again. And they laid the groundwork for a lot of other people to find happiness. Including us."

Mel grunted in partial agreement. "I guess I wouldn't exist at all if Max hadn't married

Lady Anne. So I should probably be thankful in a way."

"I know I am," said Jasper. Mel turned to see him hovering in the doorway. "I wouldn't blame you for doubting that, Mel," he said. "But do you have a minute to talk?"

Mel took a deep breath. "Sure."

Ro nodded approvingly. "I'll give you two some space."

**12**

Jasper sat down heavily at Ro's desk. "I've been a bit useless, haven't I?"

"Yeah, you have," said Mel matter-of-factly. "I know your parents think I'm just trying to get a slice of your fame and money or whatever. I'm not sure if you believe that too, or if you just decided that I'm not worth your time."

"I don't believe that," Jasper said. "But I'm ashamed to say that when I told them you'd be visiting, their reaction left me fairly shaken. I worried that I was making a mistake in bringing you here. Not because I thought you were some sort of gold digger. But because I didn't have anything of *real* value to offer you."

Mel frowned. "Meaning . . . ?"

Jasper spread his hands in a helpless gesture. "The Valmonts aren't a family. They're a business. People working together for their own benefit. Preserving their image at all costs. By the time you and I talked for the first time, I'd convinced myself that once you got to know us, you'd want nothing to do with us."

"But you invited me to Evonia anyway. And then acted super distant and weird."

"I know this isn't an excuse, but I've been terribly nervous that I would say or do something that would make you regret coming. I was afraid if I said or did anything wrong or showed you too much of the dark side of this family, you'd want to leave. And I didn't want you to leave."

Mel remained silent. She didn't know what to say to that.

"I know we can't erase the past," Jasper went on. "But we don't have to be defined by it either. I want to do better. I want to be the kind of father who can make you proud. If you'll let me try."

Mel sat with that for a minute. It wasn't a fairy tale happy ending—but it was a start. She nodded. "Okay, Dad."

Jasper smiled and took a couple of candies out of his pocket. "Hungry?'

"Yeah, I never got breakfast!"

He passed her an éclat. She unwrapped it and popped it into her mouth, savoring the bittersweetness that spread through every part of her.

**VANESSA ACTON** is a writer and editor based in Minneapolis, Minnesota. She enjoys stalking dead people (also known as historical research), drinking too much tea, and taking long walks during her home state's annual three-week thaw.